Princess Rosie's Rainbows
Text copyright © 2015 Bette Killion,
Illustrations copyright © 2015 Kim Jacobs

Library of Congress Cataloging-in-Publication Data
Killion, Bette.
Princess Rosie's rainbows / by Bette Killion ; illustrated by Kim Jacobs.
  pages cm
 Summary: "For little Princess Rosie, only rainbows could make her smile, until
a wise old woman from the farthest village teaches everyone that true happiness
doesn't come from outward possessions, but from deep within us"-- Provided by
publisher.
  ISBN 978-1-937786-44-1 (casebound : alk. paper) [1. Fairy tales. 2. Princesses-
-Fiction. 3. Happiness--Fiction. 4. Rainbows--Fiction.] I. Jacobs, Kim, 1955-
illustrator. II. Title.
  PZ8.K5255Pt 2015
  [E]--dc23
                                                                    2015016437

Printed in China on acid-free paper.
Production Date: May 2015,
Plant & Location: Printed by 1010 Printing International,
Job/Batch #: TT15040870

For information address Wisdom Tales,
P.O. Box 2682, Bloomington,
Indiana 47402-2682
www.wisdomtalespress.com

Princess Rosie's Rainbows

By

Bette Killion

Illustrated by

Kim Jacobs

❖Wisdom Tales❖

Once upon a time

in a faraway kingdom there lived a loving King and Queen. They ruled in a magical land where rainbows stretched from peak to ocean. Each day they wished for a child to share their castle.

*T*heir wish was soon granted. On a rainy summer day a daughter was born to them. The little Princess opened her eyes for the very first time. Suddenly, the sun broke through the clouds. A full rainbow appeared with bright, glowing reds. From that moment, she was truly happy only when a rainbow was in the sky.

The King and Queen named her the Princess of Rose-colored Light. But everyone called her Princess Rosie.

As she grew, she became a very serious child. She loved books and music and her dear little dog. But she often wore a frown instead of a smile—except of course when there were rainbows in the sky!

"I wish I could have a rainbow all the time," Princess Rosie often sighed.

*O*ne day the Queen sighed, too, and said, "Our Rosie is so lovely when she smiles. Her face even seems to glow. Why can't she have forever rainbows?"

"Why not, indeed!" said the King.

So he issued a notice to all people under the sky.

A BAG
OF GOLD
TO ANYONE
WHO CAN BRING
FOREVER RAINBOWS
TO MAKE OUR
PRINCESS
SMILE.

Soon great ships arrived from lands near and far. The local people greeted them with joy. Before long the road to the castle was filled with visitors. Each of them had a rainbow for Princess Rosie.

Some of the rainbows were made of silk and others of feathers. Some were made of glass and others painted. Some rainbows were printed in books and others framed in pictures. Some were made of jewels and others you could even eat!

Princess Rosie looked over each rainbow. She was polite, but at each she shook her head sadly. "They are beautiful," she said, "but they are not real. There are no softly shimmering lights. I am only happy when I see real rainbows."

The King and Queen were sad, too.

Suddenly the Queen had an idea. "Let's speak with the Royal Astronomer. Perhaps he can help our Rosie."

"I have no rainbows," said the Royal Astronomer. "But I can show you how to make them."

"How wonderful!" cried Princess Rosie.

The Royal Astronomer poured a glass of water. He then placed it on a sunny window sill.

"Now," he told Princess Rosie, "hold your hands up in front of the glass."

When she did, Princess Rosie was amazed. All the colors of the rainbow poured out onto her hands. Then she pulled her hands back. The rainbow spilled out across her white apron and skirt!

Princess Rosie smiled a wide, wide smile. The King began to reach for the bag of gold to give to the Royal Astronomer. Just then a cloud slid across the sun and the rainbow disappeared.

"Oh-h-h!" cried Princess Rosie. "I thought it was a forever rainbow, but now it is gone!"

"It is hopeless!" sighed the Queen. "We will never find what we are looking for."

A few days later an old woman came to the castle. "It is Becca, the Wise Teacher of Farthest Village," said the Queen.

Becca greeted the Queen and the Princess with a proper curtsy. "Come and sit," said the Queen. "You must be tired from your journey. Tell me, why have you come?"

"I wish to speak with Princess Rosie," Becca replied.

"Oh! Have you brought me forever rainbows?" Princess Rosie asked hopefully.

"No," said Becca, her eyes twinkling. "But I'll tell you a secret. You already have them! They are in your heart, just as everything you truly love is there also. When you feel sad or lonely simply remember the rainbows you love. Think of their glowing colors filling the sky. Soon enough rainbows will be there."

"Really?" gasped Princess Rosie.

"Yes, really!" said the wise teacher. "It is the only way to have anything forever. It doesn't rain every day. And even when it does, rainbows cannot always be seen."

"But they are in my heart because I love them?" Rosie asked.

Becca nodded. "Yes, if you can just remember!"

Princess Rosie closed her eyes. "It's true," she said. "I remembered the rainbows and now I see them!"

She smiled her biggest smile ever. Then she opened her eyes and looked up. There was only blue. No glowing rainbow colors, but she was still smiling. Princess Rosie was happy!

The good news spread quickly. All over people began to celebrate. The King presented the wise teacher Becca with a bag of gold.

"I have no need of it," she answered. "But I will take it to others who have much need. Thank you, Your Majesty." Becca blew a kiss to Princess Rosie and was gone.

To this day the King and Queen in the faraway castle are happy. And Princess Rosie is the happiest of all anytime she chooses to be.

red
yellow
blue
purple

Make Your Own Rainbow

A Simple Science Lesson

Rainbows are rays of color that form into an arc in the sky. But how are they made? Well, sunlight looks white, but it's really made up of seven different colors—red, orange, yellow, green, blue, indigo, and purple. Rainbows appear when sunlight passes through raindrops. The raindrops act like tiny mirrors, or prisms. They bend, or refract, the different colors in white light so that they become visible. The white light then spreads out into a range of colors that are reflected back to you as a rainbow.

In order for you to see a rainbow in the sky, three conditions are required. First, it must be raining somewhere close to you. Second, there must be a break in the clouds so the sun can shine through. Third, you must be positioned between the sun and the rain. If you have all three of these things, you'll be sure to see a spectacular rainbow in the sky!

You, too, can bend light into a rainbow. Like Rosie, you can make sun shine through a glass of water. Or you can shine a flashlight with a narrow beam through the glass in a darkened room. Or, outside, you can spray water from a hose with the sun behind you and look for a rainbow shining in the fine mist.

About the Author

Bette Killion is an author of poems, stories, and articles for children. She has had over 800 of them published in well-known juvenile magazines such as *Jack and Jill, Highlights, Ranger Rick, Turtle,* and *Hopscotch.* Her picture books include *The Apartment House Tree, Think of It, Just Think,* and *The Same Wind.* She is also known for her rewriting of classic fairy tales such as *Rapunzel, Beauty and the Beast,* and *Aladdin.* In addition to having built a successful writing career, Bette has also worked as a children's librarian and as a substitute teacher. She has nine grandchildren and lives in central Indiana.

About the Illustrator

Kim Jacobs has been a children's book illustrator and professional artist for over thirty years, while her popular stationery products have sold in the millions throughout the world. Her art has appeared in children's books such as *Cottage Cats: My Companions on the Path to Joy* and *Glad You are My Friend*, as well as on a wide array of gifts, toys, puzzles, fine art prints, and greeting cards. Her bestselling calendar, *The Cobblestone Way*, is now into its twenty-sixth year. Kim lives with her husband Bob in Maine, in a home powered by the sun.